THE
CHRISTMAS PARTY
FROM THE
BLACK LAGOON

THE
CHRISTMAS PARTY
FROM THE
BLACK LAGOON

HAVE A VERY SCARY CHRISTMAS!

by Mike Thaler
Illustrated by Jared Lee

SCHOLASTIC INC.

New York Toronto London Auckland Sydney
Mexico City New Delhi Hong Kong Buenos Aires

To Tina Lee,
for all her T.L.C.
—M.T.

To Jaden, Seth, and little Roman—J.L.

ISBN-13: 978-0-439-87160-0
ISBN-10: 0-439-87160-3

Text copyright © 2006 by Mike Thaler.
Illustrations copyright © 2006 by Jared D. Lee Studio, Inc.

All rights reserved. Published by Scholastic Inc.

SCHOLASTIC, Little Apple, and associated logos are trademarks and/or registered trademarks of Scholastic Inc.

33 32   17 18 19 20/0
Printed in the U.S.A.
First printing, December 2006

CONTENTS

CHAPTER 1
PLAN A

Mrs. Green says we're going to have a Christmas party. She has put everyone's name in a hat. I pulled out Penny's name.

Nobody wanted to trade me, so now she and I have to exchange presents.

I don't know what to get her, but I'm sure she'll tell me. I hope it's in my budget.

7

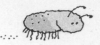

If I had picked Eric, it would have been easy. He'd want the latest *Captain Thunderpants* book, or an official whoopee cushion.

YOU'RE THE BEST, HUBIE!

LET ME READ IT.

COOL!

If it had been Freddy, his present would have been from one of four major food groups.

But Penny is a girl. I don't know what girls want. But like I said, I'm sure she'll tell me.

CHAPTER 2
HUNCH TIME

HELP!

Well, I was right. Penny sits down next to me at lunch and spends the entire noontime giving me hints. She also gives me a list just in case I missed anything. It's about four feet long.

She wants something for her Barbie collection. I make a joke, "What about some *Barbie Wire*?" . . . not appreciated. Or she wants the latest Flower Fluff Girl book, or some hair curlers.

FOUR FEET

11

NAIL
FINGER
NAIL
PINK
NAIL
POLISH

Boy, oh, boy, this is going to be an education—to say nothing about embarrassing. I'm glad she doesn't want pink nail polish, or anything with polka dots. I wish I had picked Eric.

PENNY'S LIST

PERFUME

CHAPTER 3
GO FOR BROKE

When I get home, I go over Penny's list with Mom. We ponder the problem over milk and cookies. She says when she was a girl, she liked perfume and the Beatles. Sounds like smelly bugs to me.

THE BEATLES WERE:
1. TINY CARS
2. ROCK BAND
3. PET BUGS
(ANSWER ON PAGE 16)

It's hard to picture Mom as a little girl, but she says she was one once. I'll have to take her word for it.

While munching on a chocolate chip cookie, I go confer with my piggy bank. I have exactly $2.98.

It seems I *always* have $2.98. I think I'm stuck in a financial time warp!

BOW

30" TALL →

TINY HANDS →

DAINTY FEET →

← MY MOM, A LONG, LONG TIME AGO.

CHAPTER 4
DECK THE MALL

Mom and I go to the mall. She says she'll help me shop. The mall is brimming over with Christmas spirit.

There are forty Santas—short ones, tall ones, smiling ones, and grouchy ones. There are two hundred reindeer and a thousand elves.

It's full of crisp jingles and Kris Kringles—and it's only November. Christmas seems to come earlier and earlier every year. Eventually it will start in January.

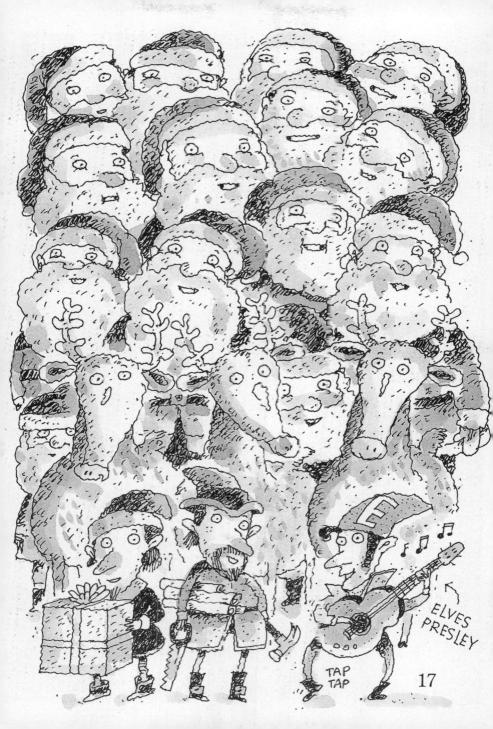

ELVES PRESLEY

TAP
TAP

17

18

We make our way to the girls'
department. I'm glad Mom is
with me.

All of a sudden, everything is
pink, fluffy, and has feathers. It's
like falling into cotton candy or
sliding down a birthday cake.
Everything has three flowers and
a bow.

Let me out! I've got to find a
dinosaur and get back to reality.

CHAPTER 5
MAULED

Well, our mall visit was not very fruitful. I felt like I was drowning in pink lemonade. Only forty-four more shopping days left till Christmas, and I still don't know what to give Penny.

Maybe I should write Dear Abby Claus, or try Googling "gifts for girls." This is silly! Why doesn't Penny just buy something she would like, and I'll get something I would like? It would be a lot simpler.

WHEN IS CHRISTMAS?
1. DECEMBER 21
2. DECEMBER 5
3. DECEMBER 25

20

(ANSWER ON PAGE 29)

21

But Mom says that's not the spirit of Christmas. She says it's about *giving*. I'm beginning to think it's about *giving up*.

CHAPTER 6
HO, HO, OH!

That evening there's a movie on the horror channel called *Santa Claws*. It's about a monster who goes out for a slay ride.

I turn to another channel. There's a musical on called *Santa Jaws*. It's about an overweight shark with a beard that goes out caroling.

HALF A BUG →

All the other channels are full of ads telling me about things I need to buy. Somehow, I don't think they've caught the spirit of the season.

↑ RING

I think Christmas should be a celebration . . . not a *sell*-ebration I press the pause button. I need a Santa *pause*.

CHAPTER 7
SCREAMIN' DREAMIN'

That night I have a dream. A singing shark is chasing me. I'm in a Santa outfit and keep tripping over my beard.

There's also a big Christmas tree ornament with a fuse, rolling after me—it's lit and sparkling.

Penny is running after me, too, waving her list. As fast as I run, they keep getting nearer and nearer. They're about to catch me . . . when I wake up sweating.

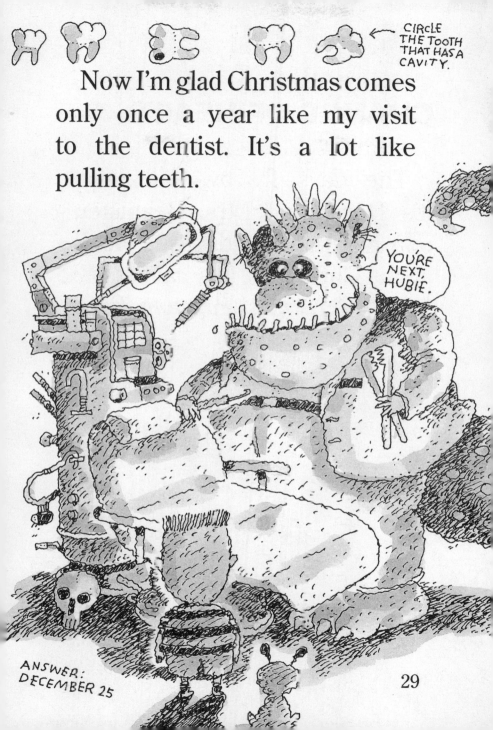

Now I'm glad Christmas comes only once a year like my visit to the dentist. It's a lot like pulling teeth.

CHAPTER 8
CHANGE OF HEART

The days fly by, and soon it's December. Mrs. Beamster, our librarian, reads us a book about Christmas. It's called *The Worst Christmas Pageant Ever.* It's funny!

In class, Mrs. Green says Christmas isn't about presents, but about kindness. She says all year people think about themselves. Then comes Christmas, and for one day, they think about others. They're polite and considerate of one another.

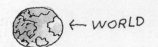 ← WORLD   BEACH BALL →

Then the day after Christmas, they are pushing and shoving to return the presents they don't want—wrong size, wrong color, wrong present.

↑
WRONG
SIZE

↑
WRONG
COLOR

Mrs. Green says if the spirit of Christmas lasted for 365 days, the world would be a better place. I bet all the shops at the the mall would agree with her.

↑
BUG

MOVE IT.
HURRY UP!
QUIT PUSHING!
WRONG SIZE.
RETURNS

CHAPTER 9
SOCK IT TO ME

Mrs. Green said we all should bring in a stocking to be filled by Santa. I looked and looked all over my house, but all I could find that was clean was a gym sock.

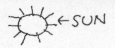 ←SUN
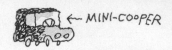 ← MINI-COOPER

Doris brought in a leotard, and Penny brought in pantyhose. But Eric brought in the biggest sock that I've ever seen. It must have belonged to a dinosaur or been an elephant's nose warmer. You could put a Mini-Cooper in it.

SPIDER →

34

Once we hung up our socks, it was time to decorate the Christmas tree. Everyone brought in an ornament we had made. I took an old tennis ball and glued buttons on it. Freddy baked a gingerbread Santa. Doris made a little ballet dancer out of ice cream sticks. And Derrick made a star for the top. Eric said he was still working on his ornament.

35

CHAPTER 10
THE TREE MUSKETEERS

Mrs. Green made a big pot of popcorn. Then we strung the pieces together and placed them on the tree. We ate as much as we decorated with.

Mrs. Beamster came in to see our tree and she read us a poem called "The Night Before Christmas." I like the part about . . . "When what to our wondering eyes did appear, but a miniature sleigh and eight tiny reindeer." She also read us a book called *The Polar Express*.

In music class, we learned all

MOLAR EXPRESS ←

the words to "Rudolph the Red-Nosed Reindeer." Then we put red balls on our noses and went to all the other classes to sing it.

Our Christmas party is four days away, and we're starting to have a ton of fun! By golly, it *is* the season to be jolly.

CHAPTER 11
THE TURNING OF THE SCROOGE

Well, I'm so confused. Is Christmas about *giving* or *living*? If it's about being nice to each other—that's easy. It doesn't cost anything to be nice.

39

The next day Mrs. Green shows us a video called *A Christmas Carol*. It's about a grumpy old man who doesn't believe in Christmas. His name is Scrooge and he only believes in money.

I ONLY BELIEVE IN CASHMAS.

Mrs. Green said, "Scrooge is a miser, who causes a lot of *miser*-y." Anyway, he gets visited by three ghosts . . . Christmas Huey, Christmas Dewey, and Christmas Louie. They give him an accounting of his life, and when he adds it up—he comes out very poorly.

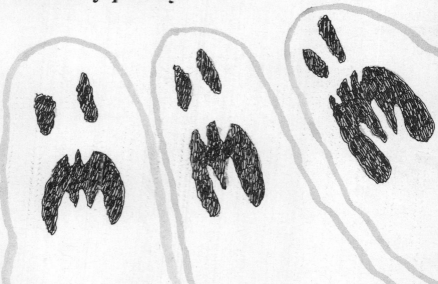

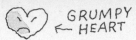 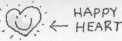

Scrooge has a change of heart and starts spending his money and his love to help other people. And finally, his *humbugs* turn into *big hugs*.

42

CHAPTER 12
THE REASON FOR THE SEASON

After watching the video, I have an idea. I raise my hand.

"Yes, Hubie?" asks Mrs. Green.

"I have an idea," I say.

"Yes?" Mrs. Green replies.

HUBIE.

43

← MONEY

"Instead of giving presents to one another," I say, "why don't we put all our money together and help people that need our help?"

Penny jumps up. "I already got you a present!" she shouts. "And you better get me one."

"That's not the point," I say. "By the way, *what* did you get me?"

↑
TINY
GIFTS

"I'm not telling," Penny says, holding up five fingers. "But it cost a lot!"

"How much?" I ask.

"Five dollars plus tax," says Penny, wiggling her fingers.

"Humbug!" says Eric, wiggling all of his.

HUGE
BUG

TINY
BUG

45

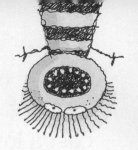

CHAPTER 13
MADE BY HAND

Well, so much for peace on Earth . . . back to the cash register, and I'm way behind. It's cash or crash!

Miss Swamp, the art teacher, suggests that we make presents for one another. That sounds good to me.

OK!

But Penny starts whining, "I already spent five dollars plus tax and my present better cost at least that."

Somehow I think we've lost the spirit of Christmas here. Then I have another idea. They say time is money. So if I spend five hours—at a dollar per hour—making Penny's present, we'll be even.

YELLOW WOOL

BRUSH

WATER

PAINT

PASTE

GYM SOCK

STRIPS OF NEWSPAPER

When I get home, I get to work.

I get papier-mâché and make a doll's head. I paint on two blue eyes and two pink lips. I use yellow wool for hair and my other gym sock for a cap.

I make a body out of a pop bottle and cover it with a piece of cloth, sort of like a dress— more like a sarong. I hope it's not *sa-wrong* dress.

CLOTH →

POP BOTTLE

PAPER →

I lose track of time and work the whole weekend on it. I take the boots off my G.I. Joe and glue them on the bottle. Then I tie on a hair bow, and I'm nearly done.

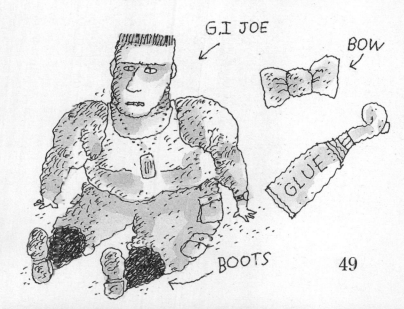

G.I JOE

BOW

GLUE

BOOTS

49

Finally I wrap the doll in pink polka-dotted paper and make up a poem on a card.

PENNY, PENNY,
I DIDN'T HAVE ANY MONEY
FUNNY
BUT I MADE THIS DOLL
MADE EVERY PART
(EXCEPT FOR THE BOOTS)
FROM MY HEART
TO YOU
MERRY CHRISTMAS,
HUBIE

I put the present on my dresser, and that night I count reindeer instead of sheep to fall asleep.

Then visions of sugar plums dance in my head. Well, they don't actually dance, they sort of roll around.

Then it begins to snow. But it doesn't snow snow, it snows popcorn. And all the trees are decorated.

When I wake up, it's Monday— the day of our Christmas party!

← POPCORN

THE SNOWMAN

CHAPTER 14
TOO MANY SANTAS

On the school bus, T. Rex is wearing a Santa cap, and when we get to school Mrs. Green is dressed up like Santa, too. So are Fester, Miss La Note, and Wanda Belch – except *her* beard is covered with a hairnet. They all go around saying, "Ho, ho, ho!"

Mrs. Beamster doesn't dress like Santa, she's dressed like an elf—a book elf. She looks more like a bookshelf.

Mrs. Swamp is dressed like a reindeer. She has wire coathanger antlers and a red ball on her nose. She tells us that she's Rudolph.

SNOW → ○

Our teachers get very silly around Christmas. I guess it reminds them of when they were kids. It's a nice thing to remember.

SNOW CONE →

CHAPTER 15
PRESENTS OF MIND

We put all the presents under our tree. Eric finally brought in his ornament. He made a Darth Vader helmet. I don't know if it catches the spirit of Christmas.

Doris is wearing mistletoe taped to her hat, and wants everybody to kiss her. No way!

MISSILE-TOE →

GEE.

KISS ME

 ← CUP

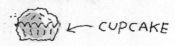 ← CUPCAKE

Freddy has baked cupcakes for the whole class, and Derrick has brought in soda pop.

Mrs. Green hands out the presents. I can't wait for Penny to open hers. There's a flurry of flying wrapping paper and a lot of *oh's* and *ah's* and a few *boos*. I hope Penny is an *oh* and not a *boo*.

I look over at her and there's a tear running down her cheek. She's hugging my doll. I hope the head doesn't fall off.

"Do you like it?" I ask.

"I love it," she says. "Where did you buy it?"

"I made it," I say proudly. She puts the doll down.

"You didn't *buy* it!" she exclaims.

"I made it," I say, "except for the boots."

"How much did it cost?" she asks.

"Nothing except time and effort," I say.

THANKS, MOM.

"Well," says Penny, coming over and taking back her gift, "I'll make *you* something, when I have the time."

Boy, I'll never understand girls, and I'll never know what she got me. But fortunately Doris got a Barbie Doll and wants to trade Penny for the doll that I made. Yay! I could kiss her . . . almost.

Penny says okay and gives me back my present. I thank her, but I don't open it. There's a boy named Tim in the special ed class. He's in a wheelchair and I'm going to give him my present.

THANKS, PAL.

They say that life is *give* and *take*. Well, from now on, I want my life to be more *give* and less *take*. And I want to celebrate Christmas every day of the year.

63